Shiva
© Demi 2020

Wisdom Tales in an imprint of World Wisdom, Inc.

Library of Congress Cataloging-in-Publication Data

Names: Demi, author.
Title: Shiva / Demi.
Description: Bloomington, Indiana : Wisdom Tales, [2020] | Audience: Ages
4-8 | Audience: Grades 2-3 | Summary: "Worshipped by millions of Hindus
worldwide, Shiva ("the auspicious one") is the god of love,
righteousness, forgiveness, longevity, protection, health, and
prosperity. He is said to bring good fortune, grace, and compassion.
Shiva is depicted as clothed in ashes, with the crescent moon crowning
his head, the holy river Ganges flowing from his matted hair, a third
eye on his forehead, a serpent around his neck, and a tiger skin around
his waist. As Nataraja, or "Lord of the Dance", he controls the forces
of creation, preservation, and destruction. Award-winning author, Demi,
presents the life and teaching of this central god within the Hindu
pantheon, replete with stunning illustrations that faithfully reflect
the ancient traditions of Hindu painting and iconography. Also included
is an appendix of Hindu prayers to the god Shiva and notes on his
representation as "Lord of the Dance""-- Provided by publisher.
Identifiers: LCCN 2019042756 (print) | LCCN 2019042757 (ebook) | ISBN
9781937786830 (hardback) | ISBN 9781937786847 (epub)
Subjects: LCSH: Siva (Hindu deity)--Juvenile literature. | Hindu
mythology--Juvenile literature.
Classification: LCC BL1218 .D44 2020 (print) | LCC BL1218 (ebook) | DDC
294.5/2113--dc23
LC record available at https://lccn.loc.gov/2019042756
LC ebook record available at https://lccn.loc.gov/2019042757

Printed in China on acid-free paper
Production Date: January 2020
Plant & Location: Printed by Everbest
Job/Batch#: 86351

For information address Wisdom Tales,
P.O. Box 2682, Bloomington, Indiana, 47402-2682
www.wisdomtalespress.com

SHIVA

DEMI*

Wisdom Tales

SHIVA is the Hindu divinity who brings good fortune, grace, and compassion. He is the god of love, righteousness, forgiveness, longevity, protection, power, health, riches, and prosperity. He wears snakes around his neck, a tiger's skin, and is covered with ashes.

He dances in cremation grounds among burning bodies.

SHIVA sits meditating on Mount Kailash in the great Himalaya mountains.

Crowned by the moon, he wears
the moon crescent in his hair, from
which flows forth the great river Ganges.

SHIVA rides on a beautiful white bull called Nandi,

and flies on a powerful green parrot named Garuda.

Brahma, Vishnu, and SHIVA are the three great Hindu gods
who create, preserve, and destroy the universe.

Brahma is the creator, Vishnu is the protector,
and SHIVA is the destroyer.

But SHIVA also has the powers
to create and resurrect.
Therefore he is said to have
all three powers of creation,
preservation, and destruction.

Parvati is SHIVA's wife, and together they are the
father and mother of the universe.

SHIVA and Parvati have two sons. Ganesha, who has an elephant head and is known as the remover of obstacles. And Skanda, who is known for his spiritual powers and healing miracles.

Once, a long, long time ago, SHIVA came to earth. Some sages and their wives were praying together, but when the wives saw SHIVA appear in all his beauty, they left their prayers and went to him.

The jealous sages decided to send a tiger to kill SHIVA.
But SHIVA easily killed the tiger with one hand and
wore it around his waist as a trophy over jealousy.

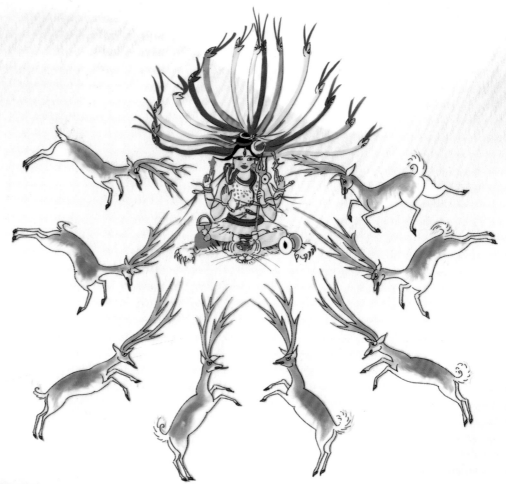

The angry sages next sent
wild deer to kill SHIVA,

but SHIVA caught them all. And the image of the deer that he holds between his two fingers is his trophy over instability.

Next, the jealous sages sent a serpent to kill SHIVA—

but SHIVA caught the snake and wore it as a trophy necklace over anger. Because of this, one of SHIVA's names is Lord of the Snakes.

The greedy sages next sent a frightening dwarf with a club to kill SHIVA. But SHIVA easily conquered the dwarf, and held him down with one foot as a symbol of his trophy over greed and illusion.

SHIVA was furious with the anger, desire, ego, greed, instability, ignorance, and jealousy in the world. And so SHIVA danced the dance of the universe: the dance of destruction, preservation, and creation.

Once there was a king named Bhagiratha, whose ancestors were sent to hell. However, he was told that if the river Ganges were to come from heaven to earth and wash away their sins, they could return to heaven. King Bhagiratha went to the river Ganges in heaven. The river said, "I can come to earth, but I will need someone powerful enough to catch and control the water's flow and not flood the earth."

King Bhagiratha thought of SHIVA and went to him. SHIVA then let down his long hair and caught the whole great river Ganges in his hair, thereby freeing the ancestors of the king, and bringing life to the earth.

One day SHIVA's wife Parvati playfully covered SHIVA's two eyes and everything became dark. So SHIVA created a third eye on his forehead so that he could always see everything: light or dark, past, present, future, and always.

Lord SHIVA has 108 Names:

The Creator, Endless and Eternal, Immovable Lord, Kind
God, Dispeller of Darkness, Conqueror of Death, Lord of the
Waters, Thunderbolt, Lord of Existence, Lord of Prosperity,
Strong One, Terrible One, Lord of the World, Lord of Time,
Lord of Mercy, Lord of Art, God of Love, etc.

Whoever chants the auspicious Names of Lord SHIVA will
be blessed by the Lord, who is capable of removing all sins.

OM NAMAH SHIVAYA!

SHIVA Prayers

All this universe is in the glory of God, of SHIVA, the God of love. The heads and faces of men are His own, and He is in the hearts of all. —*Yajur Veda*

Unequalled, free from pain, subtle, all-pervading, unending, unchanging, incapable of decay, sovereign—such is the essence of SHIVA, Lord of the summit of all paths. —*Svayambhuva Agama*

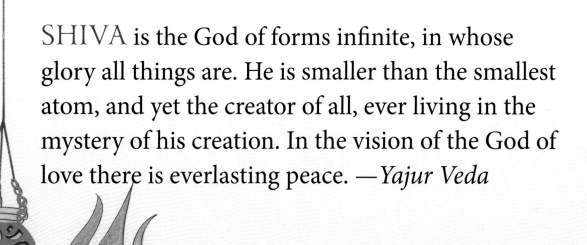

SHIVA is the God of forms infinite, in whose glory all things are. He is smaller than the smallest atom, and yet the creator of all, ever living in the mystery of his creation. In the vision of the God of love there is everlasting peace. —*Yajur Veda*

Instill in us a wholesome, happy mind, with goodwill and understanding. Then we shall ever delight in your friendship like cows who gladly rejoice in green meadows. This is my joyful message. —*Rig Veda*

SHIVA as "Lord of the Dance"

SHIVA is represented in Hindu iconography with four, eight, ten, or twelve arms. Each of his hands holds a symbolic item reflecting an aspect of his nature. For instance, SHIVA holds a trident, symbolizing his ability to create, preserve, and destroy the universe; he also holds a conch shell, symbolizing compassion; or again, a pot of water or a magic elixir, symbolizing immortality; an axe, symbolizing effort; and prayer beads, referring to the chanting of his 108 sacred Names as a means of prayer.

In his most famous depiction, SHIVA is represented as Nataraja or "Lord of the Dance." His upper arms hold respectively a drum (in the upper right hand), heralding the dance of creation; and fire (in the upper left hand), symbolizing his destruction and transformation of the universe; with his lower right hand he makes a ritual gesture of blessing to calm all fears; and with his lower left hand he points to his right foot, which is stamping on a dwarf, who symbolizes ignorance. The dance of SHIVA is thus a representation not only of the creation and dissolution of the universe, but also of his ultimate triumph over error and illusion.